GOING BACK HOME

Amish Romance

HANNAH MILLER

Tica House
Publishing

Sweet Romance that Delights and Enchants!

Personal Word from the Author

To My Dear Readers,

How exciting that you have chosen one of my books to read. Thank you! I am proud to now be part of the team of writers at Tica House Publishing who work joyfully to bring you stories of hope, faith, courage, and love.

Please feel free to contact me as I love to hear from my readers. I would like to personally invite you to sign up for updates and to become part of our **Exclusive Reader Club** —it's completely Free to join! Hope to see you there!

With love,

Hannah Miller

VISIT HERE to Join our Reader's Club and to Receive Tica House Updates:

https://amish.subscribemenow.com/

Contents

Personal Word from the Author   1

Chapter 1   4

Chapter 2   15

Chapter 3   27

Chapter 4   33

Chapter 5   38

Chapter 6   48

Chapter 7   55

Chapter 8   63

Chapter 9   70

Chapter 10   78

Chapter 11   90

Continue Reading...   93

Thank you for Reading   96

More Amish Romance from Hannah Miller   97

About the Author   99

Chapter One

Hello, Clara,

How are you doing? It's been two years now.

I cannot fully express how happy I was to receive your letter on my birthday. Danke *for the warm wishes, my dear friend. You have no idea how much I've missed you. Truth be told, when you left the community, my heart shattered at the thought of never seeing you again. Deciding to write to you turned out to be the best decision I ever made. Things might not be how we want them to be but talking to you like this is better than not at all. At least for the meantime. I truly hope you're all right.*

Everyone is fine here. Of course, we miss you. My mamm *asks about you frequently, and I will be glad to let her know you are well. I pray to Gott every day that we can meet again. But Gott knows best, and if it is his will, it'll happen.*

In other news, Jonas Garber is back in the community. I forgot to tell you in my last letter, but thankfully, I didn't forget this time. Even though I can't see your face right now, I know you gasped when you saw his name. Well, he returned alone, Clara, and although I don't know all the details, or why he left his familye, *he is back to stay. I'm sad you aren't here to see him.*

How are you? How is your familye? *How are the twins? I hope you're taking very* gut *care of them. How are Josh, Robbie, and Benny? I hope all is well, and I hope you are happy. I miss you.*

Please, write back.

Your friend,

Emily

Clara Burkholder placed the letter on her chest as she lay back on the bed. Hearing from Emily was the highlight of a stressful week. They had known each other since they were five and had been inseparable...at least until Clara's family left the faith.

A wave of sadness hit her when she thought about her former home. Two years ago, Clara was a normal Amish girl who dreamt of finding her purpose in the community and getting married to someone *Gott* had set aside for her. It was all she'd dreamed about. She loved the community, loved her life, and looked forward to joining church.

However, in the blink of an eye, her world changed completely. Her *daed* and *mamm* became weary of all the rules of the Amish community and yearned for more freedom. Clara never understood it, and after two years in the *Englisch* world, she still didn't understand it. She had been comfortable with the rules of the community, and she felt enough freedom for whatever she wanted to do. Her life had been perfect in her mind.

She rolled to her stomach and buried her head in the sheets. *Jonas Garber.* He was the first and only person who had caused her heart to flutter. Clara vividly recalled his silky, brown hair that was almost always shoved back. He hated it when his hair touched his forehead—he complained that it poked at him, so he always kept it away from his face. The look gave his face an open warmth, and Clara used to love looking at him. She loved his smile and his ocean-blue eyes.

Despite her interest in him, they had been nothing more than friends. Jonas was nice to everyone, and he treated folks with respect, so it was only typical he would be nice to her, too. They had known each other for years. And then, Jonas's family left the faith. Clara recalled how she felt the day she heard the news from Emily. It had devastated her and had convinced her they were never meant to be.

But he was back in the community now. Perhaps, it was a sign? A sign that she could return, too. She was an adult now, turning eighteen only a couple of weeks before. Hence, she could make decisions for herself. What was holding her back?

"A lot," Clara groaned, sitting up.

Her *mamm,* Freya, had recently given birth to twins. Two beautiful girls – Emma and Abby. Clara loved them dearly, and though her *mamm* tried her best with them, giving birth had taken its toll. She was exhausted. After having already given birth to Clara and her three *bruders,* it seemed as if Freya was too tired to try with the twins. Clara constantly found herself filling in for her mother's lack of care.

In truth, Clara was practically Emma's and Abby's *mamm.* She fed them, bathed them, clothed them, and put them to bed, all by herself. The only time her *mamm* put in an effort to assist with the twins was when she breastfeed them in the beginning. But that was over now, too, and the twins were fed with formula from a large supermarket nearby.

Clara understood her *mamm* spent a lot of time fussing and stewing about her other three siblings. Adjusting to their new world had been burdensome to her. There was a lot to do— like all the sporting activities Josh, Robbie, and Benny participated in. All the homework, the meetings...

It was tiring for Clara too, but she never complained. Seeing her family mostly happy compensated for her own sadness and the loss she constantly experienced. She felt out of place in their new home and had felt so from the very beginning. She wanted to return to the community she knew and had grown up in. She wanted to return to her Amish roots and faith.

And now that Jonas was back, Clara had even more reason to return.

"Clara!" her *daed* yell from down the stairs. "Clara, get down here this minute."

Clara dragged herself from the bed and trudged down the stairs. She had hoped to take a short nap since Emma and Abby were both asleep. She had barely slept a wink the night before.

"Clara?"

"I'm here, *Daed,*" she said, joining him at the foot of the stairs. "*Gude mariye.* I thought you left for work already."

Francis placed both hands on his hips. "Good morning, Clara. It's *good morning.* It's been two years, for crying out loud. How are you going to blend into this place if you're this stubborn?"

Clara swallowed. "Good morning, *Daed.*"

Francis massaged his temple. "Why are you here at home right now? What about your interview?"

Clara diverted her gaze. She had known this was coming. "Miranda said it was a waste of time."

"And just who is Miranda?"

"Our neighbor," Clara answered. "You know her. Apparently, they were going to ask for my high school diploma, and we both know I don't have one. So...there was no use."

"No use?" Francis rasped. "Weren't you the one who was so eager to get a job? That's all you've talked about. Now there's no use?"

Eager was an understatement. Clara had prayed night after night, hoping that at least one employer would look past the fact she hadn't attended a regular high school. Everywhere Clara went, the proof of graduation was demanded. The times she'd tried to explain how Amish schools worked, and she had only gotten weird stares. She had tried and tried, and now she was tired of trying. She'd run out of optimism.

"What has gotten into you, Clara?"

Clara scoffed softly. "*Daed,* I look after Emma and Abby every single day. Today, I spent all morning today bathing and feeding them as usual. *Mamm* was too tired to get up today. I had to take her meals to her, too, and then clean up the kitchen."

"So now you're complaining?"

"I'm not complaining," Clara argued. "I just...I couldn't go for the interview. After Emma and Abby fell asleep, and I put them by *mamm's* side. I thought of going for the interview. Truly, I did. But then, what was the use? I know what they were going to ask for. If I even get a job, would you let me work? Who will take care of Emma and Abby then?"

Francis sighed and paused to think. "Maybe, you're right. Maybe you should put off job seeking for now. I wasn't happy about it at first, anyway. Although, now I see what a help it might be, both to you and the family. Extra incomes are always good. But you can keep focusing on your siblings and your *mamm* for now."

Clara would have preferred that her father remain angry at her for not going to the interview, rather than be happy she wasn't job seeking anymore. He seemed more than content to have her take on all of her mother's responsibilities.

"Don't you miss home, *daed?*" Clara dared to ask.

"We *are* home," Francis answered.

"You know what I mean."

"No, I don't. We are home. This is our home, and we get to live the way we want to. I can't believe you're still pining for the district after so long."

"How else am I meant to be?" Clara asked. "I miss my friends. I miss our *haus.* I miss everything. I am completely out of place here."

"You're the one refusing to blend in," Francis lashed at her impatiently. "It's not that difficult. It's not difficult at all. Josh did it. Benny did it. Robbie did it. And they are little boys. You were sixteen when we arrived. You're eighteen now. How are you still fussing about being here?"

Clara squeezed the seam of her dress into a fist and clenched her jaw. It wasn't her fault she couldn't bring herself to like their new life. She had tried, countless times. But it was no good. She never got over her sadness. Their new life was different—too different.

"You're going to night school," Francis announced decisively. "This will help you solve two problems. It'll give you friends *and* your diploma. The last time you went to night school, you dropped out after a few days, and I let you because your mother needed you at the time. Since the high school certificate is so important, you can go to night school and get it. And by going at night, you're still free to help your mother during the day."

"What?" Clara blurted. "I don't want to go to night school..." Her mind whirled, trying to think her way out of it. Then she had an idea. "Miranda once told me I could sign up for classes online and get my diploma. I was thinking about talking to you about it. I think it sounds like a much better idea."

Francis waved his hand in the air. "You need to go to the actual school—a place where you can meet people and make friends. It will help you adjust to your life. And this *is* your life now, like it or not. The sooner you get with the program, the better."

Clara always wondered how it was so easy for everyone else to just...move on. Was she truly being dramatic, or were her feelings valid? She didn't want this life. She didn't choose this life, and she didn't want to live it.

Her first time at night school had been a nightmare. She couldn't understand a thing. It was as though they were speaking a different language. She felt so behind with no chance of catching up. Back in the community, Clara never missed a day of school. She had loved to learn. Her *mamm* used to praise her for being so inquisitive. But that had changed once they moved. Now it felt like she was being forced. *Everything* felt forced.

"I won't feel comfortable during the night classes," Clara argued. "But I do agree. I need to learn and get my diploma. I want to. But I think online classes would work best for me. I have so many things to do and going to—"

"Clara," Francis said sternly, interrupting her. "What is it about your attitude lately? You say you want the diploma, but you're refusing to go to school. You say you want a job, but you're refusing to go for interviews. There seems to be no pleasing you."

Clara stared at the ground. She had no clue why he thought she was being defensive when all she was trying to do was get him to understand.

"Goodness," Francis said with exaggerated patience. "I'm doing my best to figure you out. Yet, you argue with me at every turn. What are you thinking?"

Clara lifted her head. "I'm not arguing at every turn. I'm just saying I don't want to go to night school. I feel completely out of place there."

"And why is that?"

Clara shook her head. "I can't explain it. I just do. I'm very uncomfortable, and I feel stupid when I can't understand what they're talking about. I'm terribly far behind."

"So you have to try harder," Francis said. "I don't know. You make me weary. Maybe you're having such trouble because you're the oldest. Perhaps that's why it's harder for you. You cannot forget. We moved the family here to give you a better life. To free you from the constraints and rules the Amish community put on you. On *all* of us."

Clara held her tongue. She had never felt put upon by her Amish community.

"Your mother and I wanted more freedom, and we wanted it for you and your siblings, too. Try to understand things from our perspective. You will like it here if you gave it a try. Go to night school and make friends."

How was Clara ever going to make her *daed* understand? She loved the Amish way and wanted to live her life there, where she belonged. Besides, it was mostly older people who went to night school, and Clara didn't find the thought of making friends with them intriguing.

"*Daed,* please—"

"Enough, Clara. I'm tired of discussing it," Francis said, picking up his keys. "It's not like you have much of a choice. I've decided. You're going to night school."

Clara swallowed her words and walked back up the stairs. Was this the freedom her father wanted to give her? Forcing her to do his bidding? She blew out her breath in exasperation.

She had no plans of going to night school, and if she had to continue to argue her way out of it, then that was what she was going to do. Her schedule during the day was tedious enough. She didn't know how exactly she was going to accomplish it, but the one thing she was sure of: she wanted to marry, have children, and live the rest of her life back in the community.

Of course, it was a reality that only took place in her dreams.

Chapter Two

Your mother is very sick, Jonas. I have been writing to you, but you refuse to write back. Come home to us. She misses you. We miss you. Are you really going to ignore your sick mother when she wakes up every morning asking to see you?

I am your father, and I love you. All I want is for us to go back to being the big, happy family we were before. Your absence has created a void, one only you can fill.

Come back to us.

With love,

Your father

. . .

"*Mamm...*" Jonas mouthed.

This was the second letter Jonas had received from his *daed* in the space of one week. And it was getting to him. He was beginning to waiver. When he returned to the community, Jonas had sworn not to stay in contact with any member of his family. In truth, he wasn't supposed to be in contact with them anyway, as they were shunned after leaving the community. Besides, he was angry with them for leaving in the first place over something that might have been avoided.

But after receiving a letter from his *daed* that his *mamm* had fallen sick, Jonas was concerned for her health. He did love his parents and always wished them well. And although he couldn't speak to them, he didn't want them to suffer.

The entire wretched situation started when his *daed,* Matthew Garber, suffered continuous poor seasons on the farm. No matter what he did, or how much he did, nothing seemed to help. Jonas was old enough to see how it was affecting his *daed,* but he trusted that *Gott* would see them through. He always did.

But the situation escalated when Jonas's *daed* and his *bruders* decided to take matters into their own hands. They began to meet with people, pushing for more modern farming equipment to be allowed in the community. The other farmers – who may or may not have had success on their farms – had always survived on the equipment they'd used for generations. It was no surprise when they shut Jonas's father's ideas down without a second thought.

But Matthew was adamant. He kept going around, trying to find people who shared his opinion. Soon, his family was receiving heavy criticism and were strongly advised to desist from their actions. They became the talk of the community, and no one was on their side. The bishop became involved and there was discipline in store.

So, Jonas's father decided to leave the community. He was certain that leaving the community would be the best thing for them. He, along with Jonas's *bruders,* truly believed the community was wrong, hence, there was no place for them there.

Jonas was the only one who disagreed. The Amish ways had been the same for generations. They farmed with the same tools and equipment as always. His *daed* and *bruders* had no right to try to change the ways of the community. And the way they were stirring up controversy was wrong.

Jonas had been against his father's views from the start. But he had been expected to play the obedient son, and he had done so, even if under duress.

It had taken Jonas some time, but he was finally able to summon the courage he needed to stand up to his family. He finally told them how he felt, and that he disagreed with them. Jonas had been comfortable with his life in the community, and he had seen no reason to leave.

His views came as no surprise to his family. As expected, they tried to convince him otherwise, telling him again that it had been wise to leave. But Jonas didn't back down. Not this time. He moved back to the community and was now living with his *aenti* and her family, who were very receptive to him.

He had quickly made things right with the bishop and the church, and he had been welcomed back with open arms.

However, Jonas did not keep in touch with his family. They had not spoken for weeks. His father Matthew wrote to him regularly now, but Jonas never wrote back.

"Is something wrong, Jonas?"

Jonas snapped out of his thoughts. He stuffed the letter into his pocket and forced a smile. "Right fine, John. I was just reading a letter, that's all."

"*Ach*, is it your *familye?*" John asked, setting his hoe down.

They were out on the field working. Jonas worked hard to earn his keep. He liked it; it felt good to be working the land again as generations had before him. His fellow workers never talked about his family, nor why they had left. They didn't say a word about his *daed's* attempt to 'change the ways of the Amish' as it had been phrased.

"*Jah*," Jonas answered. "It's my *daed*. He says *Mamm* is ill."

John studied him. "Ill? You don't think it's a way to get you to come back? I... Well, I hate to say it, but maybe he ain't telling the truth. It could be his way of getting you to come back to your *familye*."

Jonas shook his head. "I don't think so. My *daed* might be a lot of things, but he wouldn't lie about something like this. He wouldn't lie about my *mamm's* health."

John shrugged his shoulders. "You can't tell. How can you be so sure? Things might have changed since you left. He might be desperate for your return."

Jonas shook his head again. His *daed* couldn't possibly lie about something like this. If he claimed his *mamm* was sick, then she was, which meant he should consider going to see her. It pained him to think of his mother ill and missing him. He wondered if he could get special permission from the bishop to go see her.

John took a step forward. "Don't tell me you're actually planning on going?"

"What? *Nee*," Jonas answered. "I-I don't know. I could visit, maybe? I wouldn't stay, of course. But I should see my *mamm* and make sure she's all right. What do you think?"

"Well, it is your *mamm*, so I understand your worry. But will you be able to go since they're shunned? I just don't know."

"I need to pray about it," Jonas said slowly. "And talk to the bishop."

John picked up his hoe again. "I still think your *daed* might be exaggerating. And your other *bruders* are there to take care of her." John swiped his perspiring forehead with the back of his hand. "What you should be worried about right now is work. *Ach*, but the sun is hot today. We need to finish, head back home, and get something to drink."

Jonas smiled and picked up his shovel. "It's true, like you say. My *bruders* are there. *Mamm* has Andrew, Gregory, and Shawn. My presence or absence won't make her well any quicker."

"That is true."

"Right." Jonas nodded, although his conscience wasn't so convinced.

"And who's to say you'd come back? Take the Burkholders for instance. They've been gone two years, and they never came back. I for one thought Clara would already be back, but she ain't here."

Clara...

Jonas smiled. "You remember Clara?"

"Of course, I remember her. She was our friend, and she lived just down the road from me."

"She used to smile all the time, *ain't so*? I remember how full of joy she used to be."

Clara Burkholder. Jonas recalled her vividly. She was one of the dear friends he'd had. Her family had left the community so suddenly, Jonas didn't even have the chance to say goodbye. He wondered where she was now and if she was happy…if she'd changed. And if she remembered him.

"Anyway, my point is, think about it before you make a rash decision, all right?"

"I will," Jonas said.

Jonas wished things could be different. There were times during the night when he would lie awake, thinking about his family. He loved them; there was no doubt about that. But they had taken a different path in life, and their paths could never meet. Jonas often said a prayer before he went to bed, asking *Gott* to bring his family back to their roots. But in truth, he had very little faith they would ever come home.

After working in the field for hours, Jonas finally called it a day. The sun was already lowering in the sky. The walk back to the house was his favorite part of each day. He liked to take the narrow path bordered by fields of grass so he could listen to the rustling. The soft brushing noise was soothing and helped him to think reflectively. How he loved working the land. Farming was in his blood.

On the other hand, John's *daed* was a carpenter these days, and he owned a small shop. He wanted John, as his eldest, to take over from him someday, and John himself had no problem with him. He had spent years learning from his *daed,* and he knew everything there was to know. Every day, after they finished working in the field, John joined his *daed* at the shop and they would finish up for the day. The only reason he still worked in the fields at all was because his father didn't yet need him full-time, and the money John earned came in handy.

Seeing John, and how he had everything set out for him, had Jonas thinking. He lived with his *aenti,* and she was a healer. Her husband was a storekeeper and had a shop in town. Jonas had no interest in any of those things. All his life, he had dreamt of owning his own farm. He always loved helping out his *daed*.

But things were different now. Jonas felt unsettled after what his family did. He couldn't explain why it affected him so much, or why it made him feel guilty, but it did.

He let out a soft sigh and stared at the sky. Working in the Kings' field might be the closest thing he would come to being a farmer.

"Why do you look so defeated, Jonas?"

The sudden sound of an elderly *mann*'s voice startled Jonas. He lifted his head, holding his breath. "Bishop Philip. I'm sorry. You startled me."

The bishop chuckled. "I didn't mean to. I was going my own way when I saw you walking with your head hanging down. I came over to see if anything was wrong. It is *gut* to have you back in the fold. I'd like to think you've adjusted to being back."

Bishop Philip stood with his hands folded in front of him. He stared at Jonas with inquisitive eyes. Bishop Philip had a long white beard, and he was a fatherly type. The community saw him as an advisor, a counselor, and a good pair of listening ears. Many went to him when they needed advice, and he was always willing and available. Jonas deeply respected the bishop.

"I'm fine, Bishop. I was just thinking," Jonas said.

"Might I ask what you were thinking about?"

Jonas scratched the nape of his neck. He decided against mentioning his mother right then, but he saw no cause not to mention his confusion with his path in life.

"I was pondering my future," he answered. "My desire to have my own farm. I would love to settle down, farm a piece of land, and have a *familye*. I need a working plan for it."

Bishop Philip nodded slowly. "What have you got so far?"

Jonas raised his eyebrows. "I'm sorry, I don't understand."

"Your plan? Have you come up with anything?" Bishop Philip asked.

"*Ach, jah...* I have a few ideas," Jonas confessed. "I'd like to purchase some land."

"What's stopping you?" Bishop Philip asked.

Jonas looked away. "A lot of things. For one, I don't have the money to start. I've been working to save, but it's growing right slow-like."

Bishop Philip tilted his head to the side. "Is that really what's bothering you, Jonas?"

It was as if the bishop could see past Jonas's forced smile. His stare was so intense, Jonas felt like the man knew what he was thinking and just wanted him to own up to it.

There was one thing further Jonas did want to bring up. "I'm worried folks might be concerned about me," Jonas said. "Because of my *familye,* Bishop."

"We have welcomed you back," Bishop Philip said.

Jonas sighed. "And I'm grateful for it. But I'm concerned folks might think I might continue where my *daed* left off. You know, try to convince them to go modern."

Bishop Philip took a step closer. "You worry about nothing. They will not think in such a way. You've come back, haven't you? You've repented. Pray about it. *Gott* will give you peace."

Jonas nodded.

"Leave all of this to *Gott.* He will show you your path. Let Him guide you in all things."

"*Danke,* Bishop," Jonas said. "There is something else I'd like to ask you about."

"Go ahead."

Jonas drew in a deep breath, summoning up his courage. "It's my ... *daed*. Or rather, my *mamm*. I received news she is very ill, and she wants to see me. I know I'm to have no contact, but I didn't know if this means in all circumstances. Going back there, even to visit, makes me uncomfortable. I don't know what to do."

Bishop Philip shook his head. "You want the hard truth, Jonas? I think you know what I will say. Your *familye* left the Amish faith and are now shunned. Let them live their lives, while you live yours. You have a community of people that accept you and won't judge you for your choices. Whatever is going on outside the community should not concern you. Do you understand?"

"Is it that simple, bishop?" Jonas whispered.

"It can be," he continued. "The one relationship you shouldn't jeopardize is the one you have with *Gott*. He will never forsake you. Focus on him and focus on your path."

Jonas forced a smile. "*Danke,* Bishop."

"If you need anything, you know where I live. Come and pay me a visit, and we can talk. Anytime."

"I'll keep that in mind. *Danke.*"

Jonas waved the bishop goodbye and continued his walk home. What concerned him was the guilt. He didn't want to be the cause of his *mamm's* suffering or get in the way of her feeling better. Jonas hated the idea that she was in pain. He had heard the bishop's opinion; one that most folks around would hold to. But he couldn't shove down the guilt.

A part of him knew his *daed* would try to make him stay if he went, but Jonas's will to remain Amish was strong and unyielding. He wasn't worried about that. He sighed heavily and continued walking home.

Chapter Three

Some days later, Jonas received another letter. He didn't want to open it, but he felt compelled to find out how his mother was doing.

Hello Jonas,

It breaks my heart that you constantly ignore my letters. I hate to believe that you would refuse your mother her wish to see you. Her illness is getting worse. Honestly, there isn't much we can do for her at this point, and it saddens me.

She has been asking for you. Her little Jonas. Although, you're not little anymore. Come home, Jonas. Come and see your mother. She misses you. I understand if you refuse to see me or your brothers. We never really agreed on things, and I know you're angry about this. But it doesn't mean you should be angry at your mother, too. She only wants what's best for all of us, and she understands that leaving the community was what was best for us all.

I don't know why you choose to stay Amish, but that's a discussion for another day.

With love,

Your father

Jonas sat at the window of the small coffee shop with a cup of tea in his hand. He had read the letter two times now. And it was as he'd feared. The same news; the same pressure. Still, the letter had its effect on him. Jonas was confused. His father was persistent, and it was beginning to weigh heavily upon him. Perhaps he needed to speak to the bishop again. Perhaps there was a way to see his mother after all.

Jonas decided to put off thinking about it for the time being. He had been hired to work for the Kings, and that was what he must do. Once he was done with his tea, he made his way down the road to the Kings' farm. He had a lot of work to finish that morning, and thankfully, the weather was nice. It was a Friday, and the thought of some rest the next day was appealing. Spending time with his *aenti* was another reason Jonas was pleased. His *aenti* loved to tell stories, and he loved to listen to them. Sometimes, he would sit and help her crush her herbs while she told him all sorts of yarns.

"Hello, John," Jonas greeted his friend as he stepped into the field. He walked over to John who was standing under a shady tree. "It's a good day to dig holes."

"Jonas—"

"I can't believe I'm so excited to get started," Jonas continued. "I think it's the weather or something. But I have a feeling it'll rain soon. Look at them clouds."

"Jonas," John said softly. "There's someone standing yonder by that tree. He's here to see you."

Jonas arched his brow. "To see me? Is it the bishop?"

"Nee," John answered. "It's actually—"

"Hello, Jonas."

That voice. Jonas didn't need to turn around to confirm it. He would recognize his *daed's* voice anywhere. John quietly left, giving them space to talk.

Jonas stared at his father in disbelief. "What are you doing here?"

"Is that the hello I get? You haven't seen me in weeks, Jonas."

"I know that, *Dat.* I'm not supposed to see or speak to you at all," Jonas said. "You know the rules. Why would you come?"

"You were not replying to any of my letters," Matthew said. "I had to come and see for myself. I thought I was writing to a ghost."

Jonas crossed his arms and sighed. "You need to leave, *daed*," he said. "I don't know why you thought it was a *gut* idea to come here, but it's not. You're only going to make things difficult for me. You need to leave."

Matthew took a step closer. "I am still your father."

"I know. But you know the rules, and I'm back here. I'm living Amish again. You know that."

"I need to talk to you. Your mother is very sick, and she needs you by her side."

Jonas squirmed. "*Jah,* I read your letters."

Matthew threw his hands in the air. "Then why haven't you come home?"

"I have considered it."

Matthew gave him a doubtful look. "Have you? Have you really considered it?"

"I have. But in truth, I-I wasn't sure. I thought maybe you were exaggerating things to get me back. I know you didn't want me to leave."

"Why on earth would I joke about your mother's health?" Matthew asked him. "Why would you think I would do such a thing? Your mother is sick, and she wants to see you. Your brothers and I want to see you, too. We want you to come home."

Jonas dropped his hands to his side. "This is the life I chose for myself, and I do not regret it. I'm not going back, *Daed.*"

"Not even for your mother?"

Jonas felt sick to his stomach. He knew how the bishop felt about things, and he didn't want to go against his advice. Still, it was his mother.

"I am considering it," he repeated.

Matthew shook his head. "You know, I'm not your enemy here, right?"

Jonas scanned the field. "No one is saying you're the enemy."

"There is no right or wrong to this. Just differing ways. We are not saying you should ignore your beliefs or lose faith. We are asking that you be with your family. You can be faithful to God and your family at the same time. There are less restrictions outside this community, Jonas. You know that. You've lived that."

"You've fully adapted to your new life," Jonas said, shaking his head. "I never did, and I don't want to. This is my home. This is my place. Stop trying to convince me like I'm the lost sheep."

Matthew sighed and took a step back. "At least come see your mother, all right? That's all I'm asking you to do. The doctors say she needs lots of rest, and she's taking her medications, but she's not getting any better. Maybe seeing you will help."

Jonas bit his lip, but he didn't say anything. He would never have guessed for a second that his father would come all the way to look for him. But he had, and now Jonas knew his father wasn't exaggerating. He wouldn't have come if his mother's illness had been a hoax.

His heart was heavy for his father was probably right. He did need to see his mother—if only just to see things for himself. He let out a sigh and shifted his weight from one foot to another. Why did everything have to be so difficult? Why did everything have to carry such consequences? He shook his head and looked again at his father.

"I will think on it," he said.

Chapter Four

"I think it's about time you started coming to the Sunday Singings. You only come to preaching service, and that's it. It doesn't feel right."

Jonas gave a laugh. "It doesn't feel right? To you?"

John nodded. "*Jah.* Don't you think it's time for you to get to know everyone again? Possibly court someone. You ain't getting any younger, Jonas."

"*Ach,* look who's speaking. You've been putting off talking to Emily for weeks. You still haven't done it, yet here you are going on about me. I tell you what... I'll follow your lead. When you summon the courage to talk to Emily, I will attend Sunday Singing."

John groaned. "You know that's not happening, right? I'm never doing it."

Jonas chuckled. "Why not? You said you prayed about it. You said you were sure she was the one. Did you forget to pray for courage, too?"

"*Jah.*" John nodded. "I don't know why it's so difficult for me to get past hello."

"Emily is your friend. We've known her for years. It can't be that hard," Jonas said.

"You can never understand. I get so tongue-tied when I try to talk to her after the singings. It's so embarrassing that I can't string together three sensible words. If you're there, maybe you can help me."

Jonah sighed and clucked his tongue. "I wish I had advice for you, John. But I don't. All I can tell you to do, is—"

"Pray about it, *jah.* I know," John said. "Come on, let's go. We'll be late for work at this point."

It was an early Monday morning. The sun shone brighter than it had in the past couple of days, but there were still plenty of clouds in the sky.

As they walked down the road, each with a cup of *kaffe* in hand, Jonas decided then and there, that he was going through with his dream. He would start his own farm like he dreamed—or at least he could start with a small piece of land.

He could expand later. In the meantime, he would continue working in the fields to make money for more land. Hopefully, what he had set aside so far was enough to get started.

Jonas thought about John's dilemma and smiled to himself. He recalled how difficult it had been for him to talk to Clara Burkholder at first, and back then, he couldn't even court her. Jonas couldn't place his finger on what it was that drew him to Clara, but he was thankful for it. Clara was bright and beautiful. She had blonde hair and light brown eyes that lit up when she smiled. Jonas recalled every detail about her face. She was the only person he had ever felt that kind of bond with. Talking to her was so easy.

"*Ach,* Jonas. He looks angry this time."

"What? Who?"

Jonas raised his head and followed John's gaze. His heart skipped a beat when he saw his *daed* approaching them with rapid, heavy steps. Jonas' eyebrow furrowed.

"*Daed...?*"

"It's happened."

His outburst caused Jonas to recoil. His father's eyes were red and somewhat swollen, but Jonas wasn't sure if it was from anger, or if he had been crying.

"*Daed,* what is it?" Jonas stuttered.

"You couldn't be bothered, could you?" Matthew whispered.

Jonas inhaled deeply. "Bothered?" he asked, but he already knew. His stomach plummeted. "It wasn't that, and you know it. In truth, I had decided to come. I was fixing to speak with the bishop about it."

"Don't bother. Your *mamm's* dead. She is gone, Jonas."

The words hit Jonas like a hammer to the chest. His heart weighed heavily, and for a moment, he thought it had stopped beating. *Dead?* So quickly? How could it be? He was going to see her.

"It–it can't be," Jonas stammered.

"All she asked was that you see her," Matthew continued. "Was it so hard for you to do? To see the person who brought you life? You broke your mother's heart. And for what?"

"But I was going to..." Jonas whispered, feeling lightheaded and ill. "I was going to come. I had it all planned out. She can't be dead."

"Well, she is."

Jonas shook his head. "*Nee.* It can't be."

Matthew took a step forward. "You had something to do with this, Jonas. If you would have come..."

Jonas kept shaking his head. "I–I'm sorry." His mind whirled to process the news. "It–it wouldn't have helped. But I could have... I should have..."

"You're too late." Matthew's words were getting to him. Jonas was shattered.

"But surely, it wouldn't have helped," Jonas whispered, trying to convince himself.

"You got your way," Matthew continued. "You didn't have to return. Now, you never have to return again. And I will never visit you again. Don't look for us, don't visit us. Since you so badly want to cut us off, then you have your wish. Your *bruders* and I will be just fine without you."

Without another word, Matthew turned on his heel and walked away, leaving Jonas heartbroken and confused. He fell to his knees with his head in his hands.

There was no way he could ever recover from this.

Chapter Five

"Abby, please fall asleep," Clara whispered. "Emma's asleep already."

Putting Abby down for her afternoon nap had become a struggle. The girl hated to fall asleep. She would stare at different things with wide eyes or cry without ceasing. Then, to make Clara's life worse, she would fall asleep a few hours before bedtime, and wake up an hour after bedtime.

Emma was the complete opposite. She loved to sleep. She would barely finish a bottle of milk before drifting off to sleep. Clara didn't want to be the type to pick favorites, but there was a clear one. Perhaps it was because Abby was the youngest, and the youngest sibling was sometimes a menace.

"Finally."

Clara cautiously set Abby down in her crib and stepped away. She assessed them, suddenly rethinking her decision. Knowing Abby, she would be awake in about thirty minutes or an hour at best, and she was going to cry. Emma on the other hand was bound to sleep for hours, but Abby's crying would wake her up.

Clara bit her lower lip.

"I shouldn't have put them close to each other," she whispered.

But it was too late to make any changes now.

Clara had just received a letter from Emily, and she was excited to read it. She hadn't heard from her in a while. So, after shutting the nursery door quietly, she hurried to her room and sat on the bed. She tore the letter open.

Dear Clara,

How are you, and how's the familye? *I received your letter about having to go to night school, and I can understand how you feel. I know I have asked this before, but why can't you just move back to the community? You're old enough to decide on your own, and I'm sure that your* familye *can survive without you.*

I miss you, Clara. You can come and stay with me and my familye *here in the community. Mamm is excited about the idea of having you here. We were always talking about attending the Sunday Singings before you left. Now, I have to go alone, and sometimes I don't feel like going at all because you're not here.*

I hope you write back with gut *news. But I'm afraid I have some bad news...*

Clara sat up straighter.

Jonas lost his mamm. *She died outside the community, but still. I heard from John, his friend, that Jonas blames himself for his* mamm's *death. You were the closest to him, so I thought you should know. He couldn't go to her funeral, and so he couldn't see her before she was laid to rest. We're trying our best to comfort him, and we're praying for him. Please keep him in your prayers, too.*

I want to know how the twins are in the next letter. Please write back.

Your friend,

Emily

"*Ach, nee.* Poor Jonas..."

Clara recalled how close Jonas had been to his *mamm*. Her death must have affected him deeply, and it must have hurt even more to not have access to her. Clara thought of Jonas's *daed*. If he had not forced Jonas to choose between family and his faith by moving away, then perhaps things might have turned out differently. Clara didn't understand how parents would train a child a certain way, then force the child to adapt differently after they had worked so hard to create a life for themselves.

Emily's offer to accommodate her if she returned to the community was tempting, and Clara wanted more than anything to accept it, but she couldn't. Not when her mother needed her so much.

Clara rose to her feet and made her way out of the house. She decided to write to Jonas and send her condolences. Jonas was her friend, after all. Clara didn't expect him to respond given what he was going through, but she wanted him to know she was praying for him.

"Clara!"

The sound of her name jolted Clara from her thoughts. She lifted her head to find Miranda waving at her from outside the gate. Clara shut the door behind her and scurried down the sidewalk. Miranda was a next-door neighbor who had been surprised to find out that a girl her age lived next door for over a year without her knowledge. Miranda had blonde hair with many layers and bangs. She liked to chew gum—incessantly, it seemed—and she always wore heavy black eye liner.

"Well, I haven't seen you in days," Miranda said. "I was beginning to think you actually got the job. Did you?"

Clara shook her head. "*Nee,* I didn't. I didn't even go to the interview. It wasn't worth it like you said."

"Still. You need to get that diploma. Have you signed up for the online classes that I told you about? Do you have a laptop?"

Clara shook her head. "My *daed* still hasn't agreed to the online classes. He wants me to go to night school."

"Gross," Miranda said. "That's old people school. Or criminals."

Clara giggled. "It's not only old people and criminals who go to night school, Miranda. But it still doesn't change the fact that I don't want to go. I get so exhausted that I can't even pay attention during night school. I think online classes are my best choice. I'll try to speak to my *daed* about it again. See if he would maybe allow me to get a laptop."

"You should. Like I said, it's hard to get a good job here if you don't have a high school diploma. I know you talked about going to school back in your community, but you need a certificate to prove it. People here don't just rely on word of mouth. Besides, you only went to age thirteen or something."

Clara nodded. "Fourteen. And I know. Believe me, I've tried to convince people before."

"Stopping so young is weird anyway. Why is that?"

Clara inhaled deeply. "Well, that's where Amish schooling stops."

Miranda scoffed. "I know, you told me, but I don't get it."

"We stop going to school at eighth grade. We believe that by that age, *kinner* have learned all there is to know to survive in the Amish community. Why bother going any further? Once you finish school, you eventually join the church. Then you mingle, meet people, court—"

"Court? Lord. You use that old-fashioned word?"

"We do," Clara said. "Courting is like your dating."

Miranda's eyebrows furrowed. "So what's the difference besides your word coming from the Dark Ages?"

"Well..." Clara pondered. "I uh – I haven't dated, so I don't know what the difference is exactly."

Miranda stared at her curiously. "Hmmm."

"Back in our Amish community, there's something called Sunday Singings. They happen after service. Preaching service is every two weeks. Anyway, after the service, later that evening, the youth meet at the same house where the service was held. Either in the barn, or a large gathering room. There we sing songs and mingle with people. If a boy likes a girl, he asks if he can take her home in his buggy." She laughed. "Of course, he'll take the long route home to give them time to chat and get to know each other.

Miranda snorted. "I like the idea of a buggy. Carry on."

"That's about it. He then takes her home."

"What? Just like that? He takes her to his house?"

"*Nee* – No, not his house," Clara explained. "He takes her home to her house."

"I see."

"When he drops her off, he might ask if she wants to go on another buggy ride, and if she does, they go on more buggy rides until he officially asks her to court."

"Have you ever courted, Clara?"

"Me? *Nee*," Clara said awkwardly. "I haven't even joined church yet."

"Why not?"

Clara cleared her throat. "Well—"

The words caught in her throat upon hearing her father's voice. Clara turned around to see him standing behind her with an accusing look on his face.

"Good afternoon, Mr. Burkholder," Miranda greeted him.

Francis forced a smile. "Good afternoon," he said then turned back to Clara. "Clara, come inside."

Clara wanted to protest, but it would be futile. Talking about life back in her old community had gotten her homesick yet again. Her father had clearly noticed and wasn't pleased.

"See you later, Clara," Miranda said.

"See you later, Miranda."

Her father didn't stop moving until he stepped into the house. Clara followed closely behind him, unsure if she should offer to take the bag he was carrying or not. He seemed annoyed, and she didn't want to anger him any further.

"What were you talking about with Miranda?" he asked, setting the bag down on the kitchen counter.

"She was asking about Sunday Youth Singings. It was nothing."

"It was nothing?" Francis asked. "You're the one who keeps complaining that you find it hard to blend in, but you decide to talk about things that would only confuse her."

Clara sighed and shut her eyes. Not this again. She couldn't do anything right in his eyes.

"Clara," Francis said, "I'm only looking out for you. I have no problem with you talking about the community with people. That's all you knew for years, and I suppose there's no harm in it. But find a better topic, and a better person to talk with."

"A better person?"

"Yes, you heard me. A better person. That girl is wild. I know her. I've seen her and the company she keeps. I don't what you around her. She is no good for you, and she will be a bad influence. I don't want that. You need to focus right now. There's a lot for you to do, and there's a lot at stake."

"*Daed—*"

"Night school, Clara," Francis cut her off. "Are you ready to sign up?"

"*Nee,*" Clara said more harshly than she should have. "I want to learn online. I promise you, I will earn the diploma. It's the same thing. I don't have to go to night school for it."

"That makes no sense. You need the actual classes, to be in front of an actual teacher. You're going to night school."

"*Daed,* I don't want to. I'm serious. This is the one thing I'm asking you. Please. It's not for me, and it's a waste of time. I won't learn that way."

Francis sighed in exasperation. "Pick one. Night school or a job. I can speak to my boss. We have gotten close, and he can get you something to do."

"But—"

"Pick one, Clara. You will not sit idle at home while everyone else is busy adapting to the town. Since you're so stubborn, I take it night school won't be your choice?"

Clara shook her head, frustrated with her father yet once again. Idle? How in the world could he possibly accuse her of being idle?

"You're getting a job, then."

Clara watched Francis walk up the stairs to his room. She dropped her head, thinking about how her already stressful life was about to get more stressful.

"*Ach, Gott* help me."

Chapter Six

"Remember, don't embarrass me, all right?" her father had warned Clara before she left to her new job.

And now she was here. It was the first time since they'd moved that she was in someone else's home. The *haus* was much bigger than theirs, and in a fancier neighborhood. Clara liked the chandelier in the middle of the room. She imagined herself lying on the floor underneath it with only its light in the room. She imagined how peaceful it would feel. Away from the noise...alone with her thoughts...

"...And make sure you come straight home after work," Francis had added. "Your *mamm* needs you to make dinner."

Clara sighed softly, remembering his stern tone. She had gotten up at four that morning when Emma had woken up screaming. Before Clara could reach their room, Emma had woken Abby up too and it had turned into a screaming competition. The only way Clara could soothe them was to feed them and hold them for over an hour. All the while, her *mamm* and everyone else slept soundly, unbothered.

"Also, remember to stop by the market before coming home," Francis had told her. "I'll see you later. Be thankful you got this job."

Clara felt a sharp pain in her head. Did her father really expect her to be thankful for the added stress to her life? Clara hated to complain, but she was on the verge of a breakdown. Not only did she have to clean their *haus,* but she also now had to clean other people's homes. Different ones, every day.

Clara sighed again and shook her head vigorously. It was time to be alert and continue her day even though she was tired. It was barely ten in the morning, but she could only think about her bed and how soft her quilt was.

"Hi, Clara," a voice said, snapping Clara back to reality.

"Hello, Mrs. Gibson," Clara greeted her. "How are you?"

"I'm very well, thank you. And you?"

"I'm well, too."

Francis had gotten Clara a job cleaning different houses in the neighborhood on different days of the week. Clara didn't like it, but she couldn't protest her *daed's* decision. Besides, making extra money wasn't such a terrible idea—she assumed she'd be able to keep a portion of her wages. If only she wasn't so tired of everything.

"Come," Mrs. Gibson said. "Let me show you to the bathroom. You will start there, and then move to the hallway and the children's rooms. Then you can clean everywhere else as you see fit. I need the bathroom cleaned before my husband wakes up."

"Yes, Mrs. Gibson," Clara said, following behind her. "I will make sure it's spotless."

"I'd appreciate that."

Clara followed her into the bathroom and stood in the middle of the ample space while Mrs. Gibson gave her instructions. Clara heard her loud and clear, but she couldn't really follow well. Her mind was all over the place as she battled her fatigue.

"Did you get all of that?" Mrs. Gibson asked after over a minute of talking non-stop.

"*Jah.*" Clara cleared her throat. "Yes, Mrs. Gibson. I'll get right to work."

"Awesome. I'll leave you to it."

Clara shut the door as soon as Mrs. Gibson stepped out and exhaled loudly. She leaned on the door's wooden panels to gather herself but instead found herself sliding down to the floor. She really wanted to shut her eyes, but she hardly had time to indulge herself with the thought of sleep, so she pushed her body back up and picked the toilet brush.

"Come on, Clara," she whispered to herself. "You always wanted a job to make some money. Now you have one. You can do this."

Feeling slightly more energetic, Clara bent over the toilet, squirted some liquid cleanser into the bowl and began scrubbing. She let her mind drift. Typically, her first thought was of Jonas, and worry clouded her mind. She wondered if he was all right. Emily had said in her last letter that he still wasn't leaving the *haus*. Clara imagined losing her *mamm*, and the thought of it was frightening.

Clara had decided to write to him, but she hadn't taken the time. Truth be told, she was skeptical about it. They hadn't spoken to each other in so long, and Clara feared Jonas had forgotten her. Her affection for him had likely been one-sided for a very long time, and it was ridiculous to expect Jonas to keep her in his heart.

"*Nee,* Clara..." she whispered.

Yet, there was no way Jonas could have forgotten her. Before she left the community, she and Jonas had been *gut* friends. Besides Emily, Jonas was the closest person to her. Even though it had been so long since they had last seen each other, the memories they made together couldn't be erased that easily, could they?

Later, after a day of cleaning, Clara trudged down the road, nearly dragging her bag on the sidewalk. She had spent the last thirty minutes at the market, shopping for the items on her *mamm's* list. Her shoulders were heavy, and her eyes were even heavier. Still, Clara felt slightly *gut* knowing she was going to get paid for the work. She had been thinking of saving money for rainy days. This was a good start. Again, she prayed her father would let her keep a portion of it.

The sound of Emma or Abby crying welcomed Clara as she walked into the *haus*. She threw her bag on the couch and walked over to the stroller.

"Hello, Abby," Clara cooed. "Hello, my love."

"Oh, *gut*. You're back."

Clara turned to the couch where Freya sat with Emma sleeping in her lap. Freya had her head on the cushion and there was a bag of chips on the couch next to her, and a glass of water in her hand.

"*Mamm,* what are you doing? Abby was crying," Clara said, patting Abby on the back.

"Well, what could I have done?" Freya asked. "If I moved, I was going to wake Emma up. Then they would both be awake and crying."

"You could have laid Emma on the couch," Clara suggested. "Abby probably has a headache from crying too much."

"Babies cry all of the time. She was going to stop eventually, and you know Abby is quite fussy."

"*Mamm*—"

"How about you take the groceries into the kitchen and start preparing dinner? Your father will be home soon, and your *bruders* are already hungry. I had to distract them with video games. Make some spaghetti."

Clara clenched her jaw. "*Mamm*, I am tired. Can we just order pizza or tacos tonight?"

"We had tacos yesterday," Freya said. "Why waste money on takeout, honey? Just make some simple spaghetti and meatballs. We're all tired, too. I took care of the babies all day long, and I just want to retire to my room and sleep."

Clara held back her snort, but she couldn't stop herself from speaking. "Well, since we're mentioning things we've done all day, I've been cleaning people's houses, and I've been up since four o'clock."

"I don't want your complaints, daughter," Freya said. "I told you before you left this morning that you were making dinner. You didn't protest then. Now, your *daed* will be back soon, and I don't want him getting annoyed. Go into the kitchen and get started."

Clara took a deep breath to calm herself. She set Abby down by Freya's side and walked into the kitchen with the bag of groceries. She was famished, hence making dinner was tolerable since she had to eat, too. But Clara hated the fact that her *mamm* thought taking care of Emma and Abby was enough work for that day. Clara had been doing that for as long as she could remember, but it was never an excuse to get out of all the other chores that had to be done.

"I can do this," she muttered with a weak smile. "After dinner, it's going to be just me and my comfortable bed for the rest of the night."

Chapter Seven

Hello, Jonas.

It saddens me to write to you after two years and under such circumstances. I am so sorry for your loss. I know how much you loved your mamm, *and I wish you didn't have to lose her. I hope you're not suffering too much, Jonas. It must have been your* mamm's *time to go, and although it's hurtful, I'm glad she is out of pain.*

I don't know what more to say. I'm hoping I don't write something that upsets you. I want you to be happy. It will be hard getting over your loss. Your mamm *loved you so much, and it would sadden her to see you too upset. Try to live happily.*

I secretly hope you haven't forgotten me, Jonas. We had a lot of memories together, many of which keep me going. You and Emily are the ones I have the best memories with.

I can't imagine you sad and in mourning. Be strong, Jonas. I wish you Gott's *love and blessings.*

You don't need to write back. I just hope that my letter helps you somehow.

With love and well wishes,

Clara

Jonas folded the letter carefully and smiled softly to himself. He would write back to her. How could he forget Clara? The one friend who could never say no to him. Recalling Clara's bright smile put one on his face. It had been really hard to smile at anything during the last two weeks, and Jonas was thankful Clara had decided to write to him.

A sigh slipped from his lips. He paused under a tree in the field and watched the other *menner* at work. He had resumed work that morning and was taking a short break. It was the first time since he received the news his *mamm* had passed away that he'd joined the others in the field. In fact, Jonas had not stepped foot out of his *haus* since then. He had no will to do anything. To eat, to get up in the morning...all he did was blame himself for everything.

But after over a week, he decided to get his life back on track. He spent time praying about it and asking *Gott* to guide him. The guilt was getting too much to bear, and Jonas was torn. A part of him hoped it wasn't his fault and that he could not have changed anything, but he couldn't help but feel terrible. It burdened him that he was unable to see his *mamm* one last time. There was the regret, the 'what if', along with his *daed's* voice in his head telling him it was all his fault.

When Jonas woke up that morning, feeling better, he decided to leave the *haus*. He made his way slowly down the road, trying to push the depressing thoughts to the back of his head. He hoped his *mamm* hadn't held a grudge against him before she passed, and he asked *Gott* for the strength to move on.

Clara was right in her letter, his *mamm* loved him deeply, and she would hate to see him give up on everything. Jonas also knew deep down that his mother had wanted to return to the community, too, but she had to stay with his *daed* and *bruders*.

Clara's letter did something for him. It was almost like a breath of fresh air. He had not heard from her in two years, and before he tore open the letter, he hadn't realized he missed her so deeply. He missed her face, he missed seeing her in the community, and he missed their talks about how they imagined life was going to be when they grew up. Jonas was turning twenty in a year, and his life was far from what he had planned it to be.

He recalled Clara's plan. She was turning twenty in two years, and he reckoned her life was not the way she pictured it to be, either. Clara had boasted she would get married at the age of eighteen to a man who loved her with all his heart. She also loved herbs, so she had claimed she would sell health mixtures to help people and to earn money. She wasn't particular about what her husband did for a living in the community. All she wanted to do was marry, have children, and be happy.

"I don't think I'm hallucinating," John said, startling Jonas. "You're smiling. *Ach, danke Gott.* Jonas is smiling."

Jonas's faint smile became slightly wider. "Don't exaggerate, John."

John stood by his side and leaned against the tree trunk. "Why are you smiling?"

"What? I can't smile anymore?"

"Well, you can." John glanced at him and sighed. "But given that the last weeks have been pure misery for you, I'm really curious. Are you all right, my friend?"

Jonas's smile waned. "I'm all right. I was just – it's Clara."

John stared at him curiously. "Clara? Clara Burkholder? What about her? Did she return or something?"

"*Nee.*" Jonas shook his head. "She sent me a letter bearing her condolences. I just recently got it, and I was remembering the silly things she used to say."

John nodded. "*Ach.* Well, if it made you smile, then I am glad Clara sent you a letter. You cannot keep blaming yourself for your *mamm*, Jonas. I really want you to feel better and move on with living your life."

"It's my *mamm* we're talking about," Jonas said, almost in a whisper.

"I know. I do know. Remember the *gut* things about your *mamm* and try to let go of the sadness of this situation. *Ach,* I might be terrible at consoling people, but you know what I'm trying to say. Your *mamm* lived a *gut* life. My *mamm* died when I was born. You know how hard it is not to think I caused the death of my own *mamm?*"

Jonas sighed and immediately felt contrite. He fiddled with his fingers, stared at John, and tried to really hear what he'd said. There were times when he couldn't tell if his friend was being serious, or if he was joking. John always went to lengths to cheer him up, and sometimes Jonas wasn't sure what was exaggerated and what wasn't.

"Well that certainly wouldn't be your fault," Jonas told him.

"You don't think that if she didn't give birth to me, she'd still be alive?"

"*Gott* gives life and takes life. It was her time to be with him, it had nothing to do with you," Jonas said.

John stayed silent for a while before he placed a hand on Jonas' shoulder. "Jonas..." he started. "*Gott* gives and takes life. You're right in that. It was your *mamm's* time to be with him. It has nothing to do with you."

Jonas felt tears sting his eyes. He shut them tightly and inhaled deeply. Earlier that morning, he had promised his *aenti* he wasn't going to mope about anymore. Jonas would try harder to dwell on the happy memories he shared with his *mamm* while ignoring the intrusive thoughts.

"So, what are you going to do now?" John asked.

Jonas rubbed his palms together. "Well, I've been thinking about things. I hope to stop working here in these fields. I have an *onkel* who asked me to come work for him on his farm quite a while back—before I even returned here. I still have a lot I want to learn as I plan to start my own farm one day. I should be able to start buying land, even if only a little at a time. Anyway, I've been thinking about a change, remembering his offer. So, I'm thinking that maybe I could start working for my *onkel* soon."

John nodded. "Sounds fine. See? It all works out well."

"Hopefully, it will." Jonas nodded. "*Danke,* John. I, well, I appreciate you more than I can say. I love you like a *bruder.*"

"I love you like a *bruder,* too." John smiled. "If you need anything, just ask me, all right? We're in this together. We've always done everything together."

Jonas gave John a punch on his arm and chuckled. They spent some time gazing at the sky, making small talk before they both went back to their day's work.

Later, the first thing on Jonas's mind was writing a letter back to Clara as soon as possible. He wanted to stay in touch with her. Even though they couldn't see each other for the time being, exchanging letters wasn't a bad idea.

Once inside his room, Jonas sat at the desk with a paper and a pen in front of him. He played with the pen for a bit, trying to come up with a response to Clara. It took him several minutes before he finally put the tip of the pen on the paper.

Hello Clara,

I cannot express how glad I was to receive your letter. I haven't heard from you in two years, and when I saw your name, I was well pleased. Danke *for the condolences.*

To be honest, my life has not been easy since I got the news of my mamm's *demise. But thankfully, with the help of John, and now, your letter, I am slowly getting out of the dark place I was in.* Danke *once again.*

How are you doing? I want to know. How is life treating you? How's your familye? *I miss seeing them. I miss seeing you. I only hope you're happy and you are still trying to achieve your dreams. Life can be tough outside the community. I know that well. But I also know that you're strong.*

Please write to me back. Tell me every eventful thing that has happened to you in the last two years. Let's start there.

Your friend,

Jonas Garber

Chapter Eight

Hello again, Clara. Thank you for your letter.

Twins?

Your mamm *had twins? Goodness! I am so happy for you all. Well, for both you and your* mamm. *I don't know why I'm excited by the news. Remember when you wanted* kinner *of your own? You used to brag that you would get married and have* kinner *that would look just like you.*

I am happy to hear that all is well with you. I also understand what you mean when you say you feel lost in your new home. I did too, but the only difference is, I finally had the courage to leave. But then, I didn't have to help take care of bopplis *like you do. My* daed, *and my* bruders *never listened to me when I spoke, and my* mamm *always took their side. It bothered me that none of them understood my yearning to return. I didn't like it, and I wasn't comfortable in that* haus, *and so I left.*

I don't regret that decision, but the thing I do regret is not seeing my mamm *before she passed away. But* Gott *knows best and I'm trying to get by every day, taking life as it comes to me.*

I truly wish I could see you, Clara.

I'm currently working on my onkel's *farm. It's* gut *hard work, and it helps take my mind off things. I'm learning a lot from him, and I plan on owning my own farm one day. Do you still want to be a healer, Clara? Or has that dream changed? Also, what are the names of the twins?*

Please write back.

Your friend,

Jonas

Clara clutched the letter tightly to her chest. She sat on a bench in the kitchen, fighting to contain her excitement. This was the third letter she had received from Jonas. Writing letters to each other was becoming a habit, like she wanted.

Suddenly, everything was more colorful, and even when she cleaned people's bathrooms, Clara hummed happy songs and caught herself almost dancing from room to room. She had read the three letters from Jonas a total of sixteen times. That too had become a habit for her. Read one in the morning, another when she got a break from work, and the last before she went to bed.

"Is that letter from Emily?"

Clara gasped and sprung to her feet immediately after hearing her *daed's* voice. She staggered a little, wondering why she felt so guilty when she had done nothing wrong.

"*Ach, nee.* It's uh—"

"From Jonas Graber, right?" he asked. "That's how many letters now? Clara, I don't want you exchanging letters with people back in the community. Emily was enough, but now you're communicating with Jonas Graber? How are you going to adjust to life here if you won't let go of the past?"

"It's not the past for me, *Daed.* It's the life I love and miss," Clara argued.

"Will you just stop?" Francis rasped. "Am I the bad person for merely wanting a better life for you and your siblings? You're the one refusing to adjust, and it isn't that things are hard for you here. You're stubbornly refusing."

Clara threw her hands in the air. "You're not like this with *Mamm,* you know? She too doesn't like this place, but she will never admit it. *Mamm* is always distraught. She too hasn't adjusted well to this fancy world we now live in. Josh, Robbie, and Benny have so many activities - sports, sleepovers, birthday parties, school activities. They keep *Mamm* frantic. She can barely keep up with it, but you don't seem to have a problem with her neglecting Emma and Abby because she is tired from carting my brothers around."

"At least your *mamm* is trying," Francis said. "What are *you* doing? Exchanging letters with the people that want nothing to do with us. You think there's a future there?"

Clara crossed her arms. "What am I doing? I don't know, maybe running this *haus?* I cook, I clean, I take care of Abby and Emma, I work. I do everything. It would be nice if you might acknowledge all of the hard work I do instead of picking a fight with me all of the time. What is so wrong in talking to my friends? Can't I do something that makes me happy? Why is that so wrong?"

Francis tightened his grip on his work helmet. "You're getting awful bold talking to me like this. I don't want you talking to that boy. Whatever it is that you both think you're doing, end it. Right now. It's no use."

"*Daed,*" Clara protested, "it's just letters. What is the harm in letters?"

"End it," Francis ordered. "You should be trying this hard to make friends here, in this place. But what do you do? You make friends with Miranda of all people. You know, I saw her smoking through our bedroom window, and I keep telling you not to hang around her, but you refuse to listen."

"Do you really think I am still at the age when I will be influenced by what a friend does?" Clara asked defensively.

"Of course, you are. You're only eighteen," Francis said. "Now, stop arguing and get to work. You've already been late once. Leave now, so you're not late a second time, and head straight home when you're done for the day."

Clara nodded, now wanting nothing more than to end this conversation. She was ashamed of how boldly she'd spoken with her father. It wasn't respectful, despite her justification. She couldn't be pleasing *Gott* with her attitude. *"Jah, Daed."*

Francis turned to walk away but stopped abruptly in his tracks. "Oh, and before I forget. You have a babysitting job on Monday. You'll be watching dogs. My boss is going on vacation, and he needed someone to watch his two dogs while he's away. Feed them, walk them, and all of that. I recommended you, and he agreed. He'll be gone only a few days, but he'll pay you well."

Clara's jaw dropped. *"Ach, daed."* She shook her head. "I can't babysit dogs."

"But you are. We've agreed on it."

"But *Daed*," Clara questioned. "I have so much work to do as it is. My schedule is full. I can't add anything else. I'm up to my neck in chores."

"It's not a difficult job," Francis insisted. "All you have to do is reduce the number of houses you clean per day to two and spread the rest out. You're not staying with the dogs. You go there every morning, feed them, take them out to go to the bathroom, walk them, set their lunch and dinner out, and go back the next day."

"*Daed,* dogs scare me."

"Goodness, Clara. Even Benny loves dogs. This is the real world. Stop complaining and giving excuses."

Clara watched her father angrily leave the *haus*. She watched him leave, puzzled. She couldn't understand it. Was he really that angry because she was afraid of dogs? Or was it because she missed her Amish friends and community? Why did he always choose to yell and get angry with her? Didn't she deserve some understanding, and not to be yelled at because she tried to explain herself.

Clara shook her head and opened Jonas's letter again. Her father had managed to ruin her mood, and she needed something to make her feel better. Luckily, she had that something in her hand.

One thing she would be forever grateful for was summoning the courage to write to Jonas in the first place. Perhaps her *daed's* worries were valid. Talking with Jonas had heightened her desire to go back home. She wanted to be with him and help him through his mourning. She wanted to go back to the *gut* times she and Jonas used to have together. She wanted to go back to the days when she perfectly timed her visits to the market to synchronize with Jonas's visit to the market. Or the times when she would lose sleep just thinking about seeing Jonas in school the next day.

Clara would do anything to get back to being her former self.

The only thing holding her back was her family. They needed her and leaving them would be harsh. Even though it was her life like Jonas had implied, she was not in complete control of it. Still, Clara wondered when the right time to break free was going to be. How long was her life going to be stuck in this excruciating loop? How long did she have to endure? And it hurt that when she spoke about it to her parents, they tagged it as complaining.

When was it going to be her turn to make her own choices? Clara felt like an eighteen-year-old, trapped in the life of a young, errant child.

Chapter Nine

"It's all right, Jonas. Clara was never shunned, so it's totally fine. You wanted to see her, and now you're already here," Jonas muttered to himself.

The spontaneous decision Jonas had made in the middle of the night had resulted in him leaving home before the break of dawn. He had tried not to think about it, until he'd arrived on Selsame Street. The very Selsame Street that was written as the return address on Clara's many letters.

"What were you thinking?" he whispered to himself as he ran his hand roughly through his hair.

Jonas wasn't thinking – or rather, he *was* thinking—of only one thing...seeing Clara. It seemed like a bad idea to search for her, but it was a much better option than lying in his pitch-black room every night, alone with his thoughts.

Writing to Clara had opened up many things in his life. Jonas anticipated her every response, he dreamt of her, and he smiled to himself whenever he recalled a memory they shared.

"I just need to see her," he told himself, walking slowly down the street. "Everything will be fine. I just need to see her."

Jonas was right that Clara was never shunned because she hadn't joined the church before her family left. She had barely turned sixteen at the time, hence she could return whenever she wanted to. But that wasn't the reason Jonas made the trip to see her. He wasn't there to convince her to come back to the community. He knew it wasn't really his business, and he didn't want to be seen as poking his nose in.

You're here because you miss her.

Jonas smiled to himself, still a bit surprised. Coming here was one of the most spontaneous things he had ever done. But something had changed in him. He felt lighter, like he was finally finding his way. Clara had said in her second letter that she missed him, too, so he wanted to believe she would be excited to see him. It *had* been two years.

As he strolled down the street, checking the houses in search for her address, he hoped his *aenti* would read his note and not worry about him. He had said he would likely to be back by nightfall, even though he wasn't sure he could make it back that day. Since the news of his *mamm's* death, his *aenti* had started to watch him closely. She worried for him—a little too much, and although Jonas was grateful, he didn't want to be a burden to her. She was already doing so much for him.

"*Ach,* heavens."

Jonas' breath caught in his throat, and he stiffened. He had been so deep in his thoughts that his heart skipped a beat when a lady who looked so much like Clara emerged from the black gate a few houses away from where he stood. She had a low ponytail, and she wore a floral ankle-length gown. Jonas peered at her, trying to get a glimpse of her face, but she wasn't looking in his direction. He quickly approached her; she was humming a song and adjusting her hair simultaneously.

"Clara?" Jonas said softly, standing a few feet away from her. "Clara, is that you?"

Jonas watched as Clara turned and her confused face slowly softened and her light brown, mesmerizing eyes widened. She gasped loudly.

"You cannot be real," she said, touching his arm. "I pray I'm not hallucinating right now because it would break my heart."

Jonas chuckled and his shoulders relaxed. "You're not hallucinating. I'm real. I'm here. I..." Jonas shook his head, puzzled. "I was looking for you, and you made this much easier by crossing my path."

"*Ach,* Jonas." Clara continued to stare at him. "You are really here? You've come to see me?"

He nodded eagerly. "I have." He chuckled. "I've missed you."

"*Ach.*" Clara hugged Jonas briefly in her excitement. She pulled away and studied his face as if she were searching for something. "You've gotten much thinner."

"I was going to say the same thing," Jonas said. "You... Well, your face looks thinner. How are you doing?"

"I am much better now you're here," she said, her voice somewhat breathless. "You missed me? I missed you, too. I miss all of you from back home, and seeing you just reminds me of—"

Clara's voice cracked. She stepped back and lowered her head. It took her a moment, but when she looked up at him, there were tears in her eyes.

"I've missed you so much, Jonas. And Emily. And John. And ... everyone. It is so lonely here," she said with a quaking voice. "I don't have many friends or anyone to talk to, and I can't seem to fit in. I only have my *familye*. You have no idea how pleased I am that you decided to come and see me."

"I'm pleased to see you, too, Clara," he said. "I'm pleased to see that you're all right. That was all I wanted to know."

Jonas was content. Seeing Clara's face with her priceless smile and glistening eyes was worth all the trouble. Her tears of happiness made his heart full. Was she really that happy to see him?

"Have you had breakfast?" Clara asked, sniffing back the tears. "I doubt you've eaten. It's still right early."

"*Ach,* not yet. I left home before the break of dawn and there was no time to stop. Where were you headed?"

"Work," she answered. "I clean a couple of homes in the neighborhood. I am also dog-sitting starting tomorrow."

"Dog-sitting? Are you? That's interesting. I never heard of such a thing. And how are Emma and Abby?" Jonas asked. "And Benny, Robbie and Josh? How are they?"

"They are well, *danke* for asking. Emma and Abby are currently asleep right now, and the boys are just ready to go to school."

Jonas looked at the house from where she'd emerged. "Your *haus* looks beautiful. It's a nice, quiet neighborhood, *ain't so?* I barely heard a peep as I walked about."

Clara nodded. "Come, let's go get something to eat. There is a nice diner around the corner that opens early. We can have fried potatoes. I know you like them."

"Wait, can I say hello to your *daed* and *mamm* first?" Jonas asked. "I feel like it's the right thing to do. Then we can go eat."

Clara bit her lip and glanced at her house. "*Ach,* well... My *mamm's* sleeping and my *daed*...well, he's getting ready for work. Let's go have breakfast first. I'm starving."

After Clara informed the two homeowners that she wouldn't be cleaning their homes until tomorrow, she and Jonas walked side by side down the street, occasionally glancing at each other. Jonas felt as if he were walking on clouds. This was the happiest he had been in a long while. He couldn't put into words how settled Clara made him feel, and although he had guessed his deep affection for her, seeing her had confirmed it.

He loved her. Plain and simple.

Like Clara had said, the diner was just around the corner. They walked in and chose a booth by the window. For the first minute, there was an awkward silence between them. They distracted themselves by staring out the window, staring at the ceiling, rapping their fingers on the table, and stealing glances at each other.

"I'll be right with you," a waitress said from behind the counter.

At last, Clara cleared her throat. "So, Jonas... How are you? I mean, really. I know the past month has been difficult for you. I'm so happy you're here so I can see you, but I fear that you remain troubled."

"I'm all right, Clara. Improved, for sure and for certain. I'm adjusting better than I did at first." He took a deep breath, not wanting to continue talking about himself. "But let's talk about you. Tell me more about your life here. Are you happy, and if you aren't, is there any way I can help?"

Clara shook her head. "I've so wanted to talk with you. I want to listen to everything you say. It's your happiness and peace of heart I want to know about."

Jonas smiled and then gave a rueful laugh. "*Ach,* Clara. I came all this way to listen to you. We'll take turns. Tell me about you, and I will tell you what you want to know afterward. We have all day. *Ach, nee,* we don't have all day. You must go to work."

"*Nee…*We do have all day. I'm going to take the day off. That's what I was telling the homeowners," Clara said, resolute.

"But Clara, will you get in trouble?"

"I don't think so," Clara said and bit the edge of her lip. "It doesn't hurt to miss one day. You came all this way to surprise me, and I plan to make the most of it."

"Well, I feel honored." Jonas said, meaning it. "Now, tell me about your life here."

Clara inhaled deeply. She was about to speak when the waitress appeared. The middle-aged lady took their order and promised to be back soon with their meal.

"Am I happy…?" Clara started, staring at her fingers. "Honest answer would be *nee,* I'm not particularly happy. Not truly. But I wouldn't say I'm sad either. I guess I'm stuck in between. I'm just living, trying to get through every day as it comes. I feel like a machine sometimes."

Jonas interlocked his fingers on the table. He remained silent, simply looking into her eyes.

Clara sighed. "I feel like I talk about it too much to my *familye*, but nobody is actually listening to me. I talk to myself a lot, more than I talk to anyone." Clara laughed lightly. "It's my way of making it through."

Jonas nodded slowly and smiled. "Me, too. I talk to myself too much. So, what are you planning to do about things? Anything?"

Clara stopped to think. "Right now, I have *nee* idea. Like I said, I feel stuck. Like I need a push to get out of this slump I'm in. But I'll figure something out eventually. I have prayed about it. I don't want to live like this forever because I don't feel *gut* about myself."

Jonas leaned in and met her gaze. "We'll figure something out. I'll help if I can. Now, tell me about the twins. Emma and Abby. I'm sure they look like you."

Chapter Ten

We'll figure something out...

It was becoming difficult to contain the butterflies in Clara's stomach. Her cheeks ached from smiling so much, but she was glad that the usual sadness she felt every morning had disappeared. It had been unbelievable at first, but Jonas was actually here to see her. Clara had no idea he cared that much about her. She had thought her love for him was one-sided, but Jonas's gaze was telling her a completely different thing.

After breakfast, they spent nearly three hours talking at the diner. Clara hadn't had a conversation like that in years. She didn't hesitate to pour her heart out to him, and she listened to Jonas narrate his experiences in the modern world before he decided to go back home. Clara envied him. The courage to leave her family and chase her own peace was what she had been begging *Gott* for.

They left the diner around noon and strolled over to a small lake in the town. It was the one place Clara liked to be; although, she didn't get there often. Not many people went there during the workday, hence it was quiet, and staring at the still water was soothing. They sat on the grass, side by side, and listened to the chirping birds. Clara had not been there in months, but she had wanted Jonas to see the lake before leaving.

Leaving...

The thought of parting again was one Clara dreaded. Being so happy today, time had passed quickly. It felt like Jonas had only been there for an hour, but it had already been nearly six.

Clara had managed to push her worries to the back of her mind. It was easy since Jonas was such a wonderful distraction. But now she imagined how furious her father was going to be when he found out she had skipped work. Even worse was that she was going around the town with the one person he had asked her to avoid. But Clara didn't care. She *couldn't* care. It was Jonas.

"I see why you like this place," Jonas said, staring at the water. "I like it."

Clara turned to him. "Do you?"

"It feels serene," Jonas continued. "I actually want to float on the water and fall asleep."

Clara giggled. "You can't fall asleep in the water, Jonas. You'd drown."

"I s'pose," Jonas said with a laugh.

He was still troubled. Clara could see it in his eyes and his demeanor. He sighed too often, and a couple of times, he feigned a smile when he noticed she was staring at him. In his second letter, he had explained all the things that had happened before his *mamm's* death. Clara feared Jonas still blamed himself.

"Jonas?" Clara said quietly. "I hate to think you might still feel guilty about your *mamm*."

"I can't seem to let it go," Jonas answered. He forced a smile while staring at the lake. "It's hard. One minute I feel like I can move on from this, and the next minute, I am saddled with guilt so heavy I can barely carry myself. There's just so much I wanted to say to her—things I should have said to her. I had planned on visiting her one last time to tell her I was happy with my life now, and I hoped she was happy with the fancy world. I never got the chance to see if she was all right, or if she truly needed me. I wanted to talk to her. And it was my fault that I was too late."

Clara placed a hand on his back. "Why not talk to her then?"

Jonas stared at her with arched eyebrows. "What do you mean?"

"Talk to her, Jonas," Clara said. "Talk to her like you believe she's listening."

"She's dead. She's gone. What's the use?"

Clara thought a moment before answering. "You need to forgive yourself, and to do that maybe you need to let go of the burden. It doesn't matter that she isn't here physically. Talk to her like she's listening, and I believe she will hear you. Say everything you want to say."

Jonas was silent as he clearly considered Clara's words. He nodded slowly and sat up. "There's so much about death we don't know. So much. I have wondered for hours about it, especially since *Mamm* has been gone. But maybe it wouldn't hurt to try."

Clara smiled. "*Gut.* I'll give you some privacy. When you're done, I'll be waiting for you by the tree. I do hope it makes you feel better."

Clara touched his shoulder lightly before she rose to her feet and walked over to a nearby tree. She sat on the grass and rested against the tree trunk, watching Jonas from the short distance. He proceeded to lower his head, and Clara could tell he was weeping, so she looked away to give him more privacy.

What Jonas had shared about his father reminded Clara of her own father. They never seemed to understand how things might be from another perspective. Or maybe they did understand, but they just chose to ignore it. It was their own way, or no way at all. No father should make his son carry the burden of his *mamm's* demise just because he chose to live differently.

After what seemed like half an hour, Jonas stood up from the grass and walked over to Clara. He stood above her for a few seconds before taking his seat by her side.

"Are you all right?" Clara asked softly.

Jonas nodded. "I guess so, but I'm not sure she heard me. I feel better though, like I have been cleansed...somehow."

"I'm glad," Clara said placing her hand over his for a moment. "I want you to be happy. You're a *gut* person."

Jonas took Clara's hand into his own and squeezed it tightly. While staring at her fingers, he drew in a deep breath and asked. "I-I love you, Clara. I have *nee* idea when I developed such deep feelings for you, but it's true. I love you, and I want to court you. I want to take you on buggy rides and someday, show the whole community just how much I care for you."

Clara forgot how to breathe for a second. Her instant response to his statement was to cry. She felt the tears quickly well up in her eyes, and they fell freely.

"I-I don't see how that's possible." Her voice broke.

Jonas's smile was gentle. "Why not? Don't you feel anything for me at all?"

"Th-that's not it. I have loved you for as long as I can remember. For years. I have imagined you courting me so many times. I could fill up pages of letters with it. But we cannot be together."

"Why not?" Jonas asked again. "Come with me, Clara. We can work something out together. I want you in my life. I promise I will only make you happy, and you will not regret choosing me."

"I'm not as strong as you," Clara said wiping her tears with the back of her hand. "I'm not as courageous. I want to go back home to the Amish where I belong, but I don't see how it's possible. I can't leave my *familye*. They need me."

He was silent for a long moment. "What about us? What about your future?" he asked softly.

"I-I will think on it," she answered, still crying. "But right now, I can't make you wait for me."

"You're not making me do anything," he said. "This is merely the start. I won't give up."

Clara didn't want him to give up, but she said nothing in response. It was getting late, and Jonas had to leave if he wanted to get back home before midnight. They walked hand in hand to her house and said the most heartbreaking goodbye to one another. Clara stood on the sidewalk and watched him walk away down the street. Her heart was heavy, and as much as she wanted to holler for Jonas to stop, she ran into her house, shut the door, and slid down to the floor.

"*Ach, Gott.* I really need your help," she whispered.

Clara felt angry and trapped, and at the same time, hopeless. This wasn't her. It wasn't the Clara she recognized. She had changed so much, and it was this place where she lived. For years, she had only endured her life there, but she didn't think it was possible to stay any longer. Jonas *loved* her. He wanted to court her. What other sign did she need to go back home?

"Clara," Francis roared, storming down the stairs. He stopped in front of her and stood with his arms flexed against his sides. "Where have you been? And what are you doing on the floor?"

Clara rose from the floor slowly and wiped her tears. "*Gut* evening, *Daed,*" she said.

"Your father asked you a question," Freya said from the living room. "Where have you been, for heaven's sake?"

Francis and Clara walked into the living room.

"I was out with Jonas," she answered her mother. "He came here to see me."

"*What?*" Francis gasped. "What did you just say?"

Clara stared at their faces and felt something shift within her. It was always going to be like this. They were never going to be content with whatever she did, unless it was exactly what they wanted her to do. They were never going to be proud of her choices or her talents.

"Actually, since you both are here, I would like to have a word with you," Clara said, taking her seat on an overstuffed chair.

"What has gotten into you, daughter?" Freya asked, sitting up straight.

Her father glared at her. "You didn't go to work today at all. How do you think that makes *me* look? Huh? Now you come back home looking like you've been on a picnic or something, and asking us to sit so you can talk?" Francis shook his head. "I s'pose now you're going to skip taking care of the dogs tomorrow."

"I told you I was terrified of dogs. Didn't I say so, *Daed?* But did you listen to me?" Clara asked. "Do you ever listen to me?"

"Clara!" her mother sputtered.

"I need to say something," Clara responded with a firm voice. "I would like to speak, too. Please sit, *Daed*. I am begging you to sit."

She had never raised her voice before, hence the shock on her parent's faces was understandable. Francis glanced at Freya who beckoned him to sit down with a gesture. Reluctant at first, he sat and crossed his arms.

"You better have a perfect explanation or excuse that you are about to give me, Clara Burkholder," Francis said, his expression set in stone.

Clara inhaled sharply, scanned their faces, and cleared her throat. "I'm sorry I raised my voice, but it was the only way I could get your attention. I-I have something to say. I want to make an announcement. I am returning home to the community. That's the only place I've ever felt happy, and I want to be happy, so I'm going home."

A thick silence ensued. Clara kept her head bowed, unable to meet their gazes. She had surprised even herself when she had said the words out loud. There was no going back from here. For months, she had prayed for the courage to speak up, and now she had. She wasn't taking it back.

Just then, she heard a sniff. Clara lifted her head and found her *mamm* at the edge of her seat, crying.

"*Ach,* Clara," she said with a quivering voice.

"I don't want to hear another word of this, Clara," Francis said. "Do you enjoy torturing your *mamm?*"

Her mother's tears pricked at her conscience, but Clara managed to keep her composure. If she didn't get her way, she was going to remain miserable for the rest of her life. From what she had seen from Jonas, living with regret wasn't pretty.

"*Daed,* I'm grown up now," Clara continued. "And I have made a decision. I'm sorry it is going to trouble you. Truly, I am. But I'm leaving."

"Are you out of your mind?" her father yelled. "And who says you can?"

"*Daed,* please. I am an adult now, and I want to go back home. I know you don't understand or approve, but I must go back. Robbie, Benny, and Josh love it here, and you can see how happy they are. When was the last time you saw me that happy about anything? Or does it not matter to you? Does my happiness not matter at all?"

"I have done *everything* for you," Francis said. "I've tried every way I can to help you adjust to our new way of life. If you would only do so, you would be just as happy as your *bruders.*"

"That's not it," Clara said. "I am not refusing. I just can't. I don't like it here. Some days I don't want to get out of bed."

"Clara," her mother said, sniffing back a sob. "Look at me, my daughter. I need you. Your *schweschder*s need you. Why don't you want to live with us?"

Clara turned to her *mamm.* "It's not that I don't want to live with my *familye.* I want to live in the community. I want that more than anything. I want my life back. I want to join church. I want to go on buggy rides with Jonas. I want to be Amish. We can work something out for you here. Miranda has a cleaner at her *haus* who is looking for more jobs. We can hire her to clean the *haus* and babysit. You don't have to do it all. I know it's hard. And I'm sorry, *Mamm.* I'm sorry, *Daed.* But I need to … do this. I need to go home. I need to breathe."

Her father rose to his feet. "You are not—"

"Francis," Freya said, lifting her hand to stop him from speaking.

They stared at each other for a long minute. To Clara's surprise, Francis sat back down and shut his eyes for a moment.

"I was afraid this day would come," Freya said softly, wiping at her eyes. "And I just didn't want it to. I've dreaded it. I don't want you to leave us."

"*Mamm,* I have to. I want to go."

"I know you do. I know. And it hurts, and we … we won't stop you. We can't, can we? Like you said, you are grown up now. You're free to go. I want you to stay. I *hope* you will stay, but you are free." She looked at her husband. "That's the way it works here in the *Englisch* world, isn't it? Daughters leave all the time."

Clara gasped and rose to her feet. "I-I can go?"

Freya sniffed and nodded. "Weren't you going to go anyway?"

"She ignores me at every turn," Francis said accusingly. It wasn't true, but Clara refused to react. And her mother was right. Her father had chosen the *Englisch* world, and daughters left all the time. But still, she wished she had his permission, or at the very least, his blessing.

Weren't you going to go anyway? her mother had asked. Clara didn't know the answer to that. She liked to think she would have the courage to leave no matter what, but in truth, she wasn't certain of it.

"*Daed?*" Clara said softly. "*Daed,* please."

Francis's sigh was loud and long. He rose to his feet and walked over to her. "It don't matter what I say, does it? My efforts mean nothing to you. They never have. Go then since that's what you want to do so badly. I won't stop you. But I'm not happy about it. It ain't right."

Despite his bitter tone, Clara hugged him and then hugged her *mamm* too. For the first time in what seemed like forever, she felt pure hope.

Chapter Eleven

Clara was *home*. It was everything she had been missing. She stood with her arms flung out and smiled sheepishly at the sky. Even though the smell of manure was strong and the chickens would not stop clucking, Clara loved it. This was home—the one she remembered and loved.

Emily had not hesitated to welcome her into their home. Her parents were as nice as they came. They set up a room for her, next to Emily's and made certain everything she needed was readily available. Emily hadn't stopped smiling since Clara had arrived the day before. They had stayed up all night talking and giggling. Clara felt alive. She would miss her family, but she would adjust.

"Do you want to go to the *kaffe* shop?" Emily asked, joining Clara by the fence. "Susan works there now, and she will be excited to see you."

Clara giggled. "*Jah*. Let's go."

"Clara!"

Clara heart raced as she turned to the road. She inhaled with joy when she saw Jonas racing in her direction.

"*Ach*, it's Jonas," Clara murmured. "Jonas is coming. Wait, how did he know I was already back?"

"I might have told John, and he might have told Jonas," Emily said slyly. "I'll leave you two alone. We're still going to the *kaffe* shop, though, *ain't so?*"

"We are," Clara said and turned back to Jonas.

"*Clara.*"

Upon reaching Clara, Jonas dropped his hands to his knees and panted. He chuckled and straightened his back, trying to catch his breath.

"You came," he said, breathlessly. "You're here."

"I am here." Clara giggled. "It's *gut* to see you, Jonas. I look forward to seeing you every day."

"Me, too." Jonas chuckled. "John told me you returned yesterday, and I couldn't believe it. Your parents let you go? You didn't run away?"

Clara leaned against the fence. "I didn't run away. After you left that day, I had the courage to tell my parents how I felt."

"What did they say?"

"They weren't happy," Clara answered. "But in the end, they accepted it. Although my *daed* couldn't look me in the eye. My *bruders*...they didn't understand why I was leaving, but they weren't upset. I'll miss Emma and Abby the most."

"I'm so happy for you, Clara. I am truly happy you're back," Jonas said. "So...can we go for that buggy ride?"

The jittery excitement was back. Clara smiled widely. "I'd like that very much."

"How does tomorrow evening suit?"

Clara nodded. "It suits right fine."

"We'll be happy, Clara," Jonas said. "I promise."

There was no better feeling in the world than the delight Clara felt at that moment. She had a future with Jonas, one she had dreamt of since she was a girl. After two long years, she was back to feeling butterflies and excitement when Jonas talked to her.

Clara was back exactly where she belonged.

The End

Continue Reading...

Thank you for reading *Going Back Home!* Are you wondering **what to read next?** Why not read *Choosing Her Beau?* **Here's a peek for you:**

Louise Lambright shuddered and squatted by the side of the one of the family goats. "What a *gut* girl. You eat well."

A cool winter wind carrying the lingering scent of wet earth blew past Louise, causing her dress to billow slightly. She reached for the strand of honey-brown hair that tickled her cheek and tucked it back under her *kapp*. She smiled, as she watched the goat gobble the rest of his feed.

"Bobby was supposed to tend all of you today, not me," Louise told the animals. "I wanted to go to the *kaffe* shop with Rebecca."

Louise groaned as she rose to her feet. She stayed until she was done feeding the goats, then she shut the barn door and walked toward the *haus*. It had snowed the day before, so the ground was slippery, and there were heaps of snow all around the *haus*. She cupped her hands over her mouth and blew hot breath on them. It helped warm them but only for a short while. Louise didn't mind. She didn't know which she loved more, winter or summer. For one, Louise loved the cold, but she didn't appreciate the below zero temperatures when it became frigid and just stepping out of the house became a daunting task. Yet, she also liked nice warm weather. But if the rain tarried for too long, the heat sometimes became uncomfortable.

The sound of someone chuckling on the other side of the fence caught Louise's attention. She stopped in her tracks and hurried over to the fence separating their *haus* from her neighbor's. She leaned on it and peered over. When she saw Mark Jones, her face widened into a smile. The hope of catching him outside his *haus* was the main reason she'd agreed to feed the goats in the first place. She had been disappointed when it appeared she wouldn't see him.

"*Gude mariye*, Mr. Jones," she beamed. "I trust you slept well."

Mark stopped his pacing and looked up at her. "Louise," he said, returning her smile.

With his warm gaze upon her, Louise' insides danced. She was reminded once again of how badly she had fallen for this

Englisch neighbor of theirs. It had started from the very first day she'd seen him. He had moved in about a year ago and mostly kept to himself. However, when she did see him, he always seemed in a jovial mood.

He had shaggy, curly blonde hair, parted down the middle, and sky-blue eyes that she got lost in whenever she spoke to him. She couldn't help but notice he was tall and well-built, with broad shoulders and an endearing smile. On top of all his fine features, he was kind, and he spoke to her and her family with respect.

VISIT HERE To Read More!

https://www.ticahousepublishing.com/amish-miller.html

Thank you for Reading

If you **love Amish Romance**, **Visit Here:**

https://amish.subscribemenow.com/

to find out about all **New Hannah Miller Amish Romance Releases! We will let you know as soon as they become available!**

If you enjoyed *Going Back Home,* would you kindly take a couple minutes to leave a positive review on Amazon? It only takes a moment, and positive reviews truly make a difference. I would be so grateful! Thank you!

Turn the page to discover more Hannah Miller Amish Romances just for you!

More Amish Romance from Hannah Miller

Visit HERE for Hannah Miller's Amish Romance

https://ticahousepublishing.com/amish-miller.html

About the Author

Hannah Miller has been writing Amish Romance for the past seven years. Long intrigued by the Amish way of life, Hannah has traveled the United States, visiting different Amish communities. She treasures her Amish friends and enjoys visiting with them. Hannah makes her home in Indiana, along with her husband, Robert. Together, they have three children and seven grandchildren. Hannah loves to ride bikes in the sunshine. And if it's warm enough for a picnic, you'll find her under the nearest tree!

Made in the USA
Middletown, DE
11 July 2022